Jolley '13

Hello Hattie!
Enjoy this
monstrous
book.
love
Rachael
Callaghan

MONSTERS UNDER BRIDGES

PACIFIC NORTHWEST EDITION

PICTURES BY **JOLBY**
WORDS BY **RACHEL ROELLKE CODDINGTON**

SASQUATCH BOOKS
SEATTLE

Manufactured in China by C&C Offset Printing Co. Ltd.
Shanghai, in January 2013

Published by Sasquatch Books

17 16 15 14 13   9 8 7 6 5 4 3 2 1

Editor: Christy Cox
Project Editor: Nancy W. Cortelyou
Illustrations and Design: Jolby & Friends
www.jolbyandfriends.com
Contributing Illustrators: Alberto Cerriteño, Eric Coddington, Rory Phillips

Library of Congress Cataloging-in-Publication Data is available.

ISBN: 978-1-57061-856-7

Sasquatch Books
1904 Third Avenue, Suite 710
Seattle, WA 98101
(206) 467-4300
www.sasquatchbooks.com
custserv@sasquatchbooks.com

MARGO THE MARIPOLO
Vancouver, BC

RONOH
Vancouver, BC

CANADA

USA

SHERMAN
Vancouver, BC /
Richmond, BC

EL DECEPCÍON
Whidbey Island, WA /
Fidalgo Island, WA

THE AURORA ZOO OF MONSTERS
Seattle, WA

Washington

IRVING THE NOBLE VEGETARIAN
Astoria, OR / Megler, WA

THE FREMONT FLIXIES
Portland, OR

PACIFIC OCEAN

LOUIS
Portland, OR

Oregon

THE SNEAKY SQUETCH
Newport, OR

KLICK AND TAT
Cascade Locks, OR

THE GRUBBEL
Lane County, OR

THE WEASLOES
Scio, OR

THE FREMONT FLIXIES

Bridge: Fremont Bridge

Location: Portland, Oregon, USA

Looks like: Round and chubby with two wings and a single eye

Diet: Salmon

Smells like: Salmon

Population: 200

Size: As round and heavy as a watermelon

Flixie   You

THE INVISIBLE HELPERS

The Flixies live within the beams of the Fremont Bridge. They share the space with a family of peregrine falcons, an endangered species. Though the Flixies are invisible most of the time, they can sometimes be seen poking their heads out from the support beams. Look closely as you drive across the bridge—especially eastbound!

When the Fremont Bridge was under construction, the Flixies realized the humans would need some help lifting the heavy steel bridge into place. They grabbed onto the bridge, clustered together, and pumped their wings to raise the bridge where it stands today, across the Willamette River.

ART NUTS!

The Flixies love art, so when they saw the beautiful arches of the Fremont Bridge, they chose it as their home immediately! They collect whatever pieces of art they can find and proudly display their collections inside their cubbyhole homes.

PORT MANN BRIDGE

PORTLY COUSINS

Every summer the Fremont Flixies visit their cousins, the Mannly Flixies, who live in the Port Mann Bridge near Vancouver, British Columbia. The Port Mann Bridge inspired the Fremont Bridge's design, so when the Mannly Flixies needed a home, the Fremont Flixies suggested they try out this Canadian bridge.

FREEWHEELIN' FLIXIES

The Flixies enjoy taking part in the Bridge Pedal, an annual event when human families ride their bikes across the bridges of Portland. Even though the Flixies can easily fly across a bridge on their own, they prefer to let the humans do all the work. They just grab ahold and ride along.

RONOH

Bridge: Ironworkers Memorial Bridge
Location: Vancouver, British Columbia, Canada
Looks like: Looks like an orca whale—big and shiny
Diet: Sea veggies and plankton
Smells like: Seaweed and wisdom
Favorite movie: *Free Willy*
Size: Heavier than 600 orca whales

Ronoh's fin   You

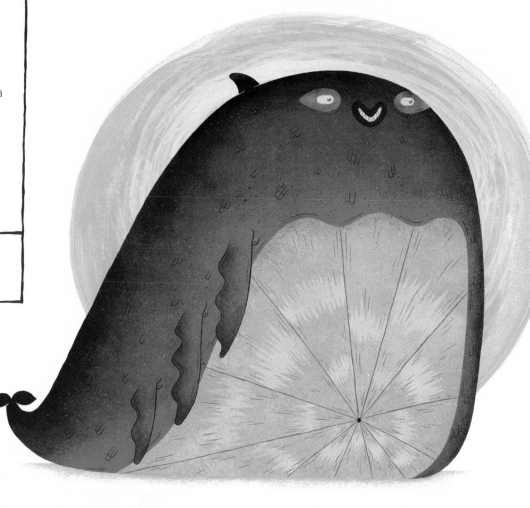

THE WISE GIANT

Ronoh, an adorable, gigantic monster, is often mistaken for a whale when the nearby whale-watching boats go by. Though he weighs more than 600 orca whales combined, only Ronoh's single tiny fin protrudes out of the water, making him seem more like an orca.

SEA KING ADVICE

Ronoh is considered one of the wisest beings in the sea. Many creatures, including the mermaids and mermen, come to him for advice. They keep it a secret, though, visiting Ronoh only at night when no one can see them. Ronoh's peaceful approach to life is widely appreciated, especially by the more nervous creatures of the sea.

FEEDING THE BEAST

Since his hunting skills have diminished over the years, the great Ronoh gets his food delivered to him by the community of sea creatures to whom he gives advice.

LOUIS

Bridge: St. Johns Bridge
Location: Portland, Oregon, USA
Looks like: Long, birdlike legs and scaly wings
Favorite snack: Doughnuts
Favorite author: J. K. Rowling
Size: As skinny as a broom

Louis's legs   You

THE TALL TRAVELER

Louis is a monster who enjoys traveling. He grew up in a military family, constantly moving from place to place. As a child he loved exploring the great outdoors, as well as the buildings in all the places he lived.

HOME AWAY FROM HOME

St. Johns Bridge in Portland, Oregon, is designed to look like the beautiful arches of Europe's Gothic cathedrals. In fact, the park and neighborhood near the bridge are named Cathedral Park. The bridge reminds Louis of the time he spent in Europe, and gives him a sense of peace.

LOUIS'S PARENTS

MONSTER PASSPORT
USA

12 COLOGNE, GERMANY
13 PARIS FRANCE
Florence ITALY

BRIDGE PERCH

Louis loves to sit cross-legged at the top of the bridge and look out across the Willamette River. The fresh breeze and occasional drizzle inspire him, so he writes frequently in his journal when he's here. Though he returns every few months to enjoy the bridge and visit his Northwest monster friends, his true home is the open road.

SWEET TREATS

Louis loves doughnuts. He has been known to gather up an entire boxful from a variety of shops in Portland, perch atop the bridge, and munch happily while ships and cars pass beneath him.

KLICK AND TAT

Bridge: Bridge of the Gods
Location: Cascade Locks, Oregon, USA
Looks like: Half beaver, half fish
Diet: Turtles and wood
Smells like: Fish
Favorite game: Tug-of-war
Size: As tall as a 6th grader

Klick   Tat   You

BROTHERLY LOVE

Two monster brothers, Klick and Tat, live beneath the Bridge of the Gods in Cascade Locks, Oregon. When they were young, they both fell in love with the same monster girl. Though she has since moved to Fresno, California, the boys continue to fight over her.

BROTHERS AT PLAY

Boys will be boys, and these monsters are no exception. They love to play practical jokes on each other. When you see water splashing against the rocks beneath the bridge, it may very well be the brothers at play.

NATIVE LEGEND

Coincidentally, there is a Native American legend about the Bridge of the Gods that follows a similar story and goes like this: Two brothers, Pahto and Wy'east, both fell in love with a beautiful woman named Loowit, who guarded a natural land bridge. They fought over her with fireballs and earth-quaking blows.

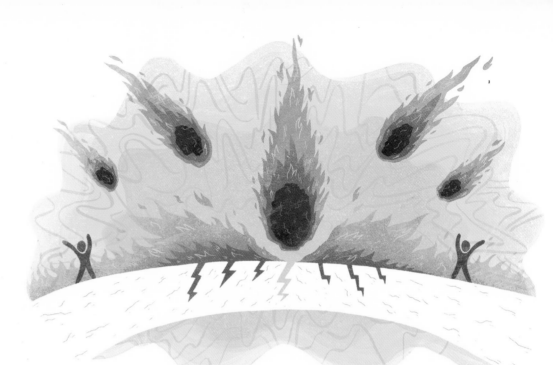

Their father, Sahale, was very disappointed in his sons. He destroyed the bridge, which fell into the river below, then turned Wy'east into Mount Hood and Pahto into Mount Adams. The maiden Loowit turned into Mount St. Helens. Humans rebuilt the bridge out of steel in 1926 and named it after the fallen bridge as a tribute to the legend.

IRVING THE NOBLE VEGETARIAN

Bridge: Astoria-Megler Bridge

Location: Astoria, Oregon, and Megler, Washington, USA

Looks like: Luscious brown fur and lots of muscles

Diet: Local, organic vegetables

Smells like: Vegetables and hair gel

Pet peeves: Cruel humans and fur coats

Size: As big as a bounce house

Irving   You

THE PROTECTOR

Irving, an old vegetarian monster, saw the deaths of many furry friends in the 1800s when the fur trade was in full swing. In his anger, he destroyed the fur-trade ships as they sailed into the Columbia River. Eventually the fur companies went out of business. Nowadays, Irving guards the Astoria-Megler Bridge, which crosses the mouth of the Columbia River.

EAT YOUR VEGGIES

Irving is a vegetarian and prides himself on eating locally sourced produce and dairy products. His animal friends help him gather food, and in exchange, he keeps an eye on them.

21,474 FEET LONG (THAT'S A LOT OF SARDINES!)

WASHINGTON

BEASTLY BEAUTY

Because of the thick fog and moisture in the air, Irving spends many hours primping and preening in order to keep his fur looking beautiful and healthy.

FOG: FRIEND OR FOE?

The fog that damages Irving's hair helped him destroy the fur-trade ships. It hid him from view, adding an element of surprise toward the unsuspecting fur traders.

THE AURORA ZOO OF MONSTERS

Bridge: Aurora Bridge
Location: Seattle, Washington, USA
Population: 19

WELCOME TO THE ZOO!

The Aurora Zoo of Monsters is located underground, beneath the Aurora Bridge in Seattle, Washington. Monster Trixie Fremont, and her husband, Jojo, gathered up the collection and went about searching for a safe place to display these endangered creatures of the monster world. When Trixie discovered the human-built stone troll—grasping a real VW Beetle—located beneath the bridge, she knew she'd found the right spot for the entrance! She hired monsters who could create an entire zoo underground.

From the Spleeack to the Boonie Bears to the Palonius Bunks, these monster creatures are housed safely for all to enjoy—all monsters, that is! Monsters travel from around the universe to view this famous collection.

AURORA BRIDGE

FREMONT TROLL

GUNDDLE DUNN

CHOMP CHAMPS

THE NYKLOP

THE SPLEEACK

PAPA MERMMY

THE SNEAKY SQUETCH

Bridge: Yaquina Bay Bridge

Location: Newport, Oregon, USA

Looks like: Long and lean with handlike scales along his back

Diet: Junk food and rocks

Most prized possession: Suzie Boonie's secret diary

Size: As thick as an elephant, as long as the Yaquina Bay Bridge

Squetch   You

STOLEN TREASURES

The Yaquina Bay Bridge in Newport, Oregon, is home to the Sneaky Squetch, a tricky monster obsessed with human belongings. Many humans have lost important items (canoes, cell phones, hamsters, flip-flops) from right under their noses when they crossed this bridge. The Squetch is not an evil-spirited monster; he simply loves the thrill of chasing cars and collecting human items.

WINDOWS UP

When crossing the Yaquina Bay Bridge, it is recommended that you keep your windows rolled up and your belongings in your lap. Make sure any items on top of your car are SECURELY fastened. Though the Squetch is sneaky, his arms are (usually!) not strong enough to unlatch car racks.

HANDS-ON

The Squetch's snakelike body easily slides beneath the arching curves of the bridge. The handlike scales along his back help him do two things: hold onto the bridge, and snatch items from the cars of unsuspecting humans crossing overhead.

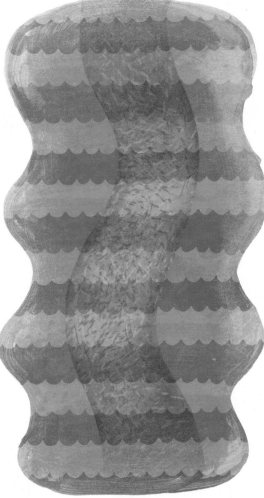

BLENDING IN

The Squetch is capable of changing color, so at times he is difficult to see. However, if you look closely, you can catch glimpses of his shiny scales beneath the waves of the bay.

THE WEASLOES

Bridge: Scio Covered Bridges

Location: Scio, Oregon, USA

Looks like: Long, furry body with large ears and anywhere from one to four eyes

Diet: Clothing, nothing sweet

Smells like: Dirt and wood

Favorite pastime: Catching snakes

Size: As fat as a Labrador retriever, as long as a car

Weasloe   You

BRIDGE BUDDIES

In the Pacific Northwest there is a species of monster, the Weasloe, that loves dark, cool, damp places—in particular, covered bridges. In Scio, Oregon, there is a set of five covered bridges that are famous places for spotting the pesky Weasloe monsters.

LOOK-ALIKE

The Weasloe is frequently mistaken for the Dumbo rat, a rodent with big ears also commonly found in the Pacific Northwest. However, Weasloes are much longer, with even larger ears, and, occasionally, extra eyes.

SUGARY DEFENSE

Weasloes are not dangerous, but they are incredibly annoying and known to eat through entire suitcases of clothing. When parking near the bridges of Scio, it is advised to drizzle soda or juice around the car; Weasloes have an extreme distaste for sugar.

HANNAH BRIDGE

SHIMANEK BRIDGE

GILKEY BRIDGE

THE GRUBBEL

Bridge: Cape Creek Bridge

Location: Lane County, Oregon, USA

Looks like: Droopy skin, warts, spiky tail

Diet: Garbage and prunes

Smells like: Pipe smoke and dirty socks

Favorite muffin: Blueberry

Size: As tall as a Ferris wheel, as fat as a rhino

The Grubbel   You

TWO HEADS ARE BETTER THAN ONE

This concrete bridge on the Oregon Coast Highway, marked by its 220-foot arch, is called the Cape Creek Bridge. Underneath it resides a rare, two-headed monster: the Grubbel.

OPPOSITES ATTRACT

The Grubbel is one of the oldest monsters in existence. He is characterized by his flabby skin, warts, spiky tail, and two heads that do not get along; they spend most of the time arguing over silly things.

PENGUIN SIGHTINGS

Local wildlife in the surrounding Devils Elbow State Park includes the common murre, which looks like a penguin. About twice a week, one of the heads, named Murray, insists that he sees a real penguin. The other head, Marvin, argues endlessly about the impossibility of a penguin living in the mild climate of the Oregon Coast.

NOISE POLLUTION!

The one thing Murray and Marvin agree on is road noise. Both heads are bothered by the sound of cars rumbling over the bridge, so the Grubbel plugs all four of his drooping ears with clothes and garbage.

HECETA HEAD LIGHTHOUSE

THE GRUBBEL GHOST

Nearby, the Heceta Head Lighthouse keeps watch over the water below. Legend has it that a ghostly woman haunts the keepers' quarters. It's really the Grubbel, searching for something to plug his ears.

MARGOT THE MARIPOLO

Bridge: Capilano Suspension Bridge
Location: Vancouver, British Columbia, Canada
Looks like: Small and fuzzy with incredibly ornate wings
Diet: Insects and berries
Favorite pop singer: Justin Bieber
Size: As light as a feather, as big as a flower

Margot   You

FIRST FLIGHT

Much like butterflies, Maripolos spend their childhood as slimy, wormlike bugs. Once they reach adulthood, they crawl to the top of the Capilano Suspension Bridge's rope handrail to take their first flight together. One day each year you can see immense numbers soar from the bridge.

FEAR OF FLYING

One particular Maripolo, Margot, has lived her whole life without fluttering into adulthood. She sadly watched each of her brothers and sisters take flight into the evergreen beauty below, while her multicolored wings remained unused by her side.

MARIPOLO METAMORPHOSIS

GOO

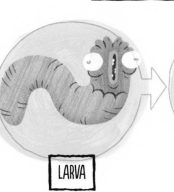

LARVA

NAPTIME!

MARIPOLO

FRIENDS IN NEED

Despite the encouragement Margot gets from her woodland friends, she has yet to gain the courage to fly. Each time a person walks across the bridge, she cringes, frightened by the motion.

MARGOT

A HIDDEN BLOSSOM

At times, Margot's curled-up body is mistaken for a flower, growing nearby the bridge.

EL DECEPCÍON

Bridge: Canoe Pass and Deception Pass Bridges
Location: Whidbey Island and Fidalgo Island, Washington, USA
Looks like: Unknown
Diet: Unknown
Size: Unknown

El Decepcíon?

???

⚊ You

BEFORE THE BRIDGE

A narrow channel of whirling, swirling water, known as Deception Pass, lies between Fidalgo and Whidbey Islands in Washington State. In the early 1900s, human travelers who needed to cross this channel had to use a ferry—which they called to service by banging a saw with a mallet! The humans soon realized they needed a faster and easier way to travel between the two islands, so they built a bridge across the pass.

FIDALGO ISLAND

PASS ISLAND

WHIDBEY ISLAND

CANOE PASS BRIDGE

DECEPTION PASS BRIDGE

SEA CREATURE DISCOVERY

During the bridge's construction, the humans discovered the remains of an old Spanish ship that had crashed hundreds of years earlier. Among the remains were drawings of a large petrified sea creature lying in the water between the two islands. The humans realized they were building the middle of the bridge, which consists of two spans, across the back of this ancient monster.

THE DRAWINGS OF EL DECEPCÍON

The sketches show an immense, turtlelike monster labeled "El Decepcíon." One of the oldest sketches includes a message explaining the monster was turned to stone by higher gods as punishment for being troublesome to the humans when they entered the water.

SHERMAN

Bridge: North Arm Bridge

Location: Vancouver and Richmond, British Columbia, Canada

Looks like: Lightbulb-shaped body with huge eyes

Diet: Astronaut meals and milkshakes

Smells like: Cardboard and cinnamon

Favorite house of Hogwarts: Gryffindor

Size: As tall as you

Sherman | You

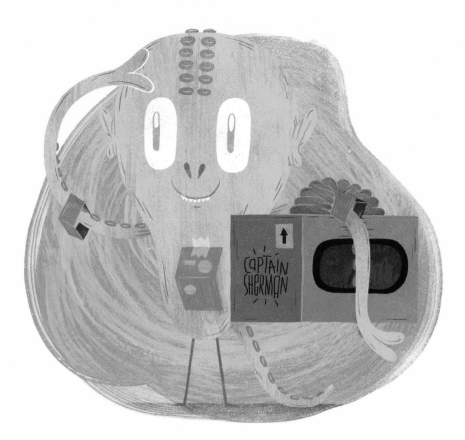

CANADA'S SMARTEST MONSTER

Sherman, the self-proclaimed "smartest monster in Canada," makes his home beneath the incredible North Arm Bridge in Vancouver, British Columbia. This bridge is for SkyTrains; no cars allowed! There is also a pathway attached to one side of the bridge that's just for bicyclists and pedestrians—that's where Sherman lives.

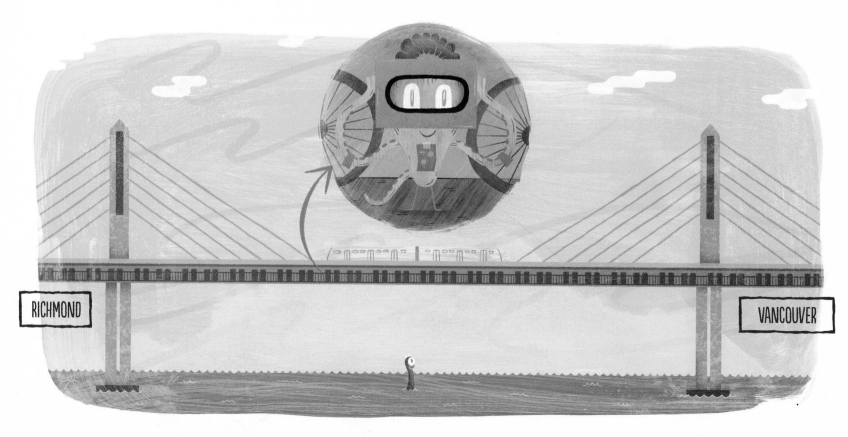

RICHMOND

VANCOUVER

PLANET SPLARK

A TICKET TO SPLARK

This imaginative monster loves science fiction and is inspired by the futuristic look of the SkyTrains. Though he was born and raised in Vancouver, Sherman insists that he's from the alien planet Splark. He plans to travel back there one day, and is in the process of creating a spaceship using spare bike parts and cardboard boxes.

ENDURANCE TRAINING

Sherman is in training for his big flight back home. Once every couple of weeks he straps himself to the front of the SkyTrain and rides it across the bridge. He says he is "building tolerance" to strong winds and high speeds.

ABOUT THE AUTHOR & ARTISTS

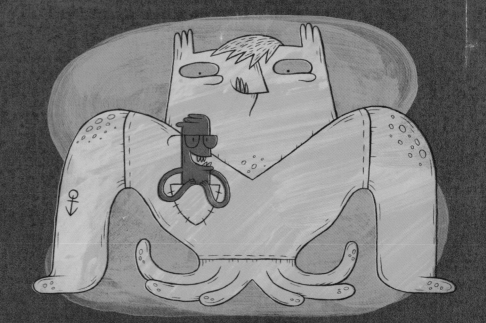

RACHEL ROELLKE CODDINGTON
AUTHOR

Rachel lives in Portland, Oregon, with her husband, Eric. She was born and raised in Fresno, California, as a part of a huge, loving family. She has been writing stories and poems for a very long time. In addition to writing, she loves singing, beatboxing, handcrafting flowers from paper, and enjoying the Pacific Northwest.

www.sunnyandstumpy.com

JOLBY (JOSH KENYON & COLBY NICHOLS)
ILLUSTRATORS / DESIGNERS

Jolby is a collaborative design and illustration studio based in Portland, Oregon. Josh and Colby combine their talents as art directors, designers, and illustrators. Their illustrations have been exhibited in galleries all over the world. They have two goals for every piece of work they create: "Tell a memorable story" and "Make people smile."

www.jolbyandfriends.com

CONTRIBUTING ARTISTS

El Decepcíon, page 27 (in order from top to bottom, left to right):
Rory Phillips - www.gogopicnic.com
Jolby - www.jolbyandfriends.com
Alberto Cerriteño - www.albertocerriteno.com
Eric Coddington - www.ephalo.com

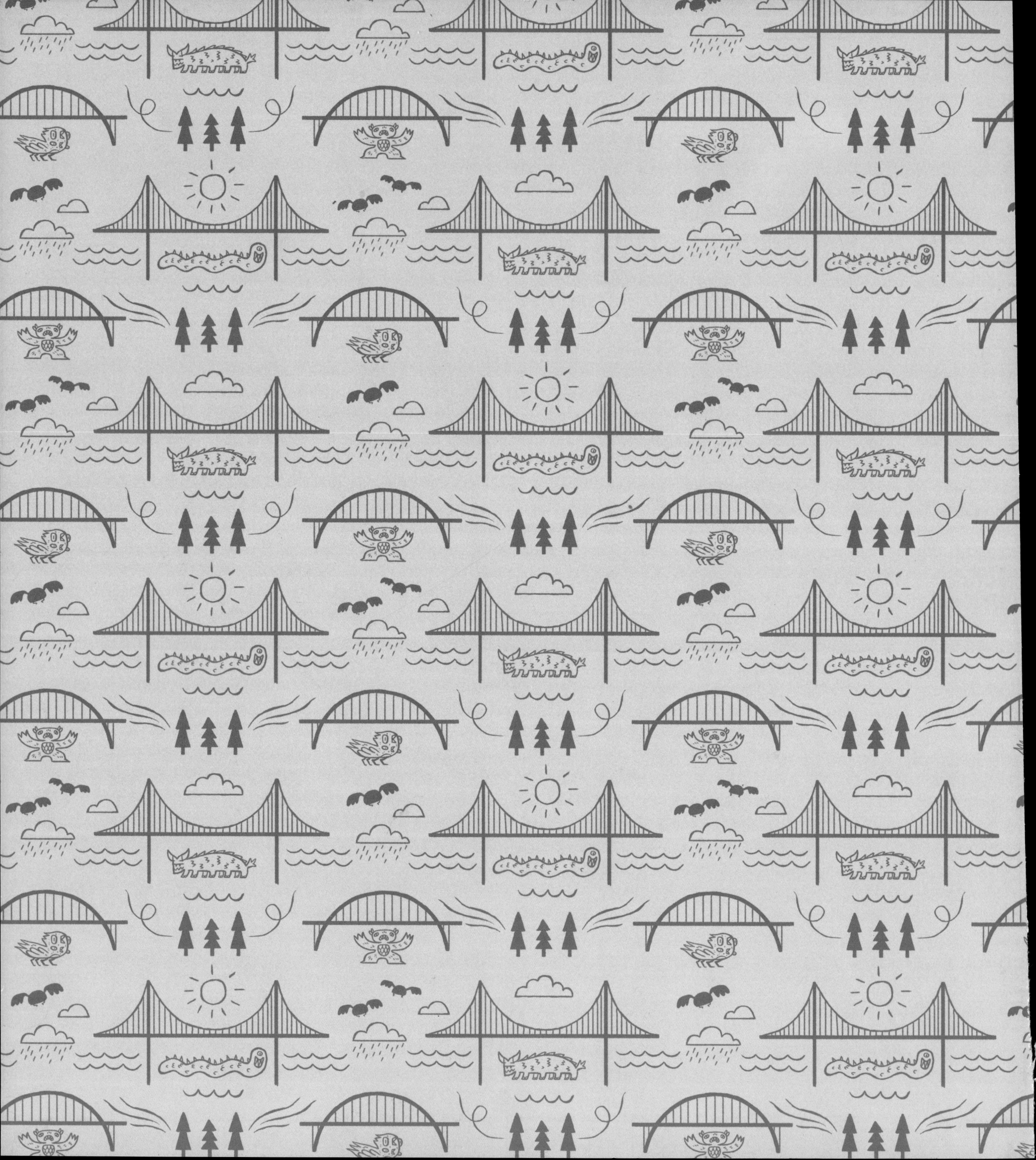